Dear Parents:

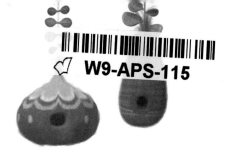

Congratulations! Your child is taking the first steps on an exciting journey. The destination? Independent reading!

STEP INTO READING® will help your child get there. The program offers five steps to reading success. Each step includes fun stories and colorful art or photographs. In addition to original fiction and books with favorite characters, there are Step into Reading Non-Fiction Readers, Phonics Readers and Boxed Sets, Sticker Readers, and Comic Readers—a complete literacy program with something to interest every child.

Learning to Read, Step by Step!

Ready to Read   Preschool–Kindergarten
• big type and easy words • rhyme and rhythm • picture clues
For children who know the alphabet and are eager to begin reading.

Reading with Help   Preschool–Grade 1
• basic vocabulary • short sentences • simple stories
For children who recognize familiar words and sound out new words with help.

Reading on Your Own   Grades 1–3
• engaging characters • easy-to-follow plots • popular topics
For children who are ready to read on their own.

Reading Paragraphs   Grades 2–3
• challenging vocabulary • short paragraphs • exciting stories
For newly independent readers who read simple sentences with confidence.

Ready for Chapters   Grades 2–4
• chapters • longer paragraphs • full-color art
For children who want to take the plunge into chapter books but still like colorful pictures.

STEP INTO READING® is designed to give every child a successful reading experience. The grade levels are only guides; children will progress through the steps at their own speed, developing confidence in their reading.

Remember, a lifetime love of reading starts with a single step!

DreamWorks Trolls © 2016 DreamWorks Animation LLC. All Rights Reserved. Published in the United States by Random House Children's Books, a division of Penguin Random House LLC, 1745 Broadway, New York, NY 10019, and in Canada by Penguin Random House Canada Limited, Toronto, in conjunction with DreamWorks Animation LLC.

Visit us on the Web!
StepIntoReading.com
randomhousekids.com

Educators and librarians, for a variety of teaching tools, visit us at RHTeachersLibrarians.com

ISBN 978-0-399-55903-7 (trade) — ISBN 978-0-399-55905-1 (ebook)
ISBN 978-0-399-55904-4 (lib. bdg.)

Printed in the United States of America
18 17 16 15 14 13 12 11 10

DREAMWORKS

TROLLS

ALL ABOUT the TROLLS

by Kristen L. Depken

Random House New York

Welcome to Troll Village!
It's the coolest place
to sing, dance,
and eat cupcakes!

There are friendly Trolls
of all shapes and sizes.
They all have awesome talents
and make Troll Village special.

This is Poppy!

She is the perky princess of Troll Village.

Poppy is bright and cheerful!

She loves to sing and dance.

She also loves to hug.

She hugs her friends

every hour on the hour!

Branch is gray and grumpy.

Branch is always worried.

He lives by himself

in a super-secret bunker.

Branch does not like

singing or dancing.

He is definitely *not* a hugger.

Cooper has pink striped fur.

He plays the harmonica

and loves to dance.

He is the most playful

Troll around.

Cooper likes to go wild
on all four legs.

Sweet Biggie is the biggest Troll
and has the biggest heart.
He is almost eight inches tall!
Biggie has a cute best friend
named Mr. Dinkles.
He loves to dress Mr. Dinkles
in cute outfits.

Satin and Chenille are fashion twins.

They are connected by their hair.

Satin is pink. Chenille is blue.

They make super-stylish outfits

for every Troll Village event.

They may look alike,

but they never dress alike!

DJ Suki is the Troll Village music mixer.
She brings her own music
to every party.

This is Guy Diamond!
He never wears any clothes
but is covered in glitter
from head to toe.
His glitter brings
a sparkle to any party!

Maddy works hair magic!

She runs the hair salon.

She helps every Troll

look amazing.

Creek is cool and calm.

He is a great yoga teacher,

a groovy dancer,

and a kind friend.

He always knows what to say

to cheer up the other Trolls.

Meet Fuzzbert!

He is hard to understand

through all that hair,

so the Trolls just have to guess

what he is saying.

Smidge is a tiny Troll
with a big voice.
She is very fit,
thanks to her favorite hobby—
lifting weights with her hair!

Harper loves to paint.

Her hair is the best paintbrush!

Paint flies everywhere

when she creates amazing art!

Karma loves camping,

climbing trees,

and playing with critters.

They love playing

in her garden of hair!

Cybil is the wisest troll

in Troll Village.

She is a great listener,

but her advice can be a little silly.

Not everyone is
as happy as the Trolls.
The Bergens are
unhappy creatures.

They think eating Trolls
will make them happy.

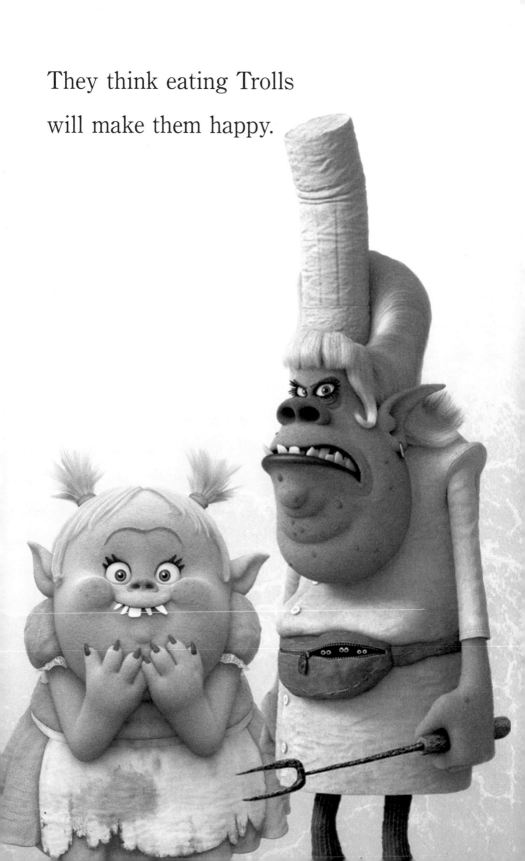

King Gristle is the king

of Bergen Town.

He wants to bring happiness

to his kingdom—with Trolls.

He can't wait to eat one!

Chef is a whiz in
the Bergen Town kitchen.
Her favorite Troll recipes
are Trollcakes
and Egg Trolls.

Bridget is a maid

in the kitchen of the castle.

She is sweet and kind.

No one pays attention to Bridget.

Then the Trolls give her

a makeover.

She becomes the fancy

Lady Glittersparkles!

Poppy and her friends teach
the silly Bergens how to be happy
without eating Trolls.

Poppy wants
everyone to share
their true colors!